SNOW WHITE

AND OTHER EXAMPLES OF JEALOUSY UNREWARDED

Amelia Carruthers

Origins of Fairy Tales
from Around the World

CONTENTS

An Introduction to
The Fairy Tale

Fairy Tales are told in almost every society, all over the globe. They have the ability to inspire generations of young and old alike, yet fail to fit neatly into any one mode of storytelling. Today, most people know these narratives through literary works or even film versions, but this is a far cry from the genre's early development. Most of the stories began, and are still propagated through oral traditions, which are still very much alive in certain cultures. Especially in rural, poorer regions, the telling of tales – from village to village, or from elder to younger, preserves culture and custom, whilst still enabling the teller to vary, embellish or adapt the tale as they see fit.

To provide a brief attempt at definition, a fairy tale is a type of short story that typically features 'fantasy' characters, such as dwarves, elves, fairies, giants, gnomes, goblins, mermaids, trolls or witches, and usually magic or enchantments to boot! Fairy tales may be distinguished from other folk narratives such as legends (which generally involve belief in the veracity of the events described) and explicitly moral tales, including fables or those of a religious nature. In cultures where demons and witches are perceived as real, fairy tales may merge into legends, where the narrative is perceived both by teller and hearers as being grounded in historical truth. However unlike legends and epics, they usually do not contain more than superficial references to religion and actual places, people, and events; they take place 'once upon a time' rather than in reality.

The history of the fairy tale is particularly difficult to trace, as most often, it is only the literary forms that are available to the scholar. Still, written evidence indicates that fairy tales have existed for thousands of years, although not perhaps recognized as a genre. Many of today's fairy narratives have evolved from centuries-old stories that have appeared, with variations, in multiple cultures around the world. Two theories of origins have attempted to explain the common elements in fairy tales across continents. One is that a single point of origin generated any given tale, which then spread over the centuries. The other is that such fairy tales stem from common human experience and therefore can appear separately in many different origins. Debates still rage over which interpretation is correct, but as ever, it is likely that a combination of both aspects are involved in the advancements of these folkloric chronicles.

Some folklorists prefer to use the German term *Märchen* or 'wonder tale' to refer to the genre over *fairy tale,* a practice given weight by the definition of Thompson in his 1977 edition of *The Folktale.* He described it as 'a tale of some length involving a succession of motifs or episodes. It moves in an unreal world without definite locality or definite creatures and is filled with the marvellous. In this never-never land, humble heroes kill adversaries, succeed to kingdoms and marry princesses.' The genre was first marked out by writers of the Renaissance, such as Giovanni Francesco Straparola and Giambattista Basile, and stabilized through the works of later collectors such as Charles Perrault and the Brothers Grimm. The oral tradition of the fairy tale came long before the written page however.

Tales were told or enacted dramatically, rather than written down, and handed from generation to generation. Because of this, many fairy tales appear in written literature throughout different cultures, as in *The Golden Ass,* which includes *Cupid and Psyche* (Roman, 100–200 CE), or the *Panchatantra* (India, 3rd century CE). However it is still unknown to what extent these reflect the actual folk tales even of their own time. The 'fairy tale' as a genre became popular among the French nobility of the seventeenth century, and among the tales told were the *Contes* of Charles Perrault (1697), who fixed the forms of 'Sleeping Beauty' and 'Cinderella.' Perrault largely laid the foundations for this new literary variety, with some of the best of his works including 'Puss in Boots', 'Little Red Riding Hood' and 'Bluebeard'.

The first collectors to attempt to preserve not only the plot and characters of the tale, but also the style in which they were told were the Brothers Grimm, who assembled German fairy tales. The Brothers Grimm rejected several tales for their anthology, though told by Germans, because the tales derived from Perrault and they concluded that the stories were thereby *French* and not *German* tales. An oral version of 'Bluebeard' was thus rejected, and the tale of 'Little Briar Rose', clearly related to Perrault's 'The Sleeping Beauty' was included only because Jacob Grimm convinced his brother that the figure of *Brynhildr*, from much earlier Norse mythology, proved that the sleeping princess was authentically German. The Grimm Brothers remain some of the best-known story-tellers of folk tales though, popularising 'Hansel and Gretel', 'Rapunzel', 'Rumplestiltskin' and 'Snow White.'

The work of the Brothers Grimm influenced other collectors, both inspiring them to collect tales and leading them to similarly believe, in a spirit of romantic nationalism, that the fairy tales of a country were particularly representative of it (unfortunately generally ignoring any cross-cultural references). Among those influenced were the Norwegian Peter Christen Asbjørnsen (*Norske Folkeeventyr*, 1842-3), the Russian Alexander Afanasyev (*Narodnye Russkie Skazki*, 1855-63) and the Englishman, Joseph Jacobs (*English Fairy Tales*, 1890). Simultaneously to such developments, writers such as Hans Christian Andersen and George MacDonald continued the tradition of penning original literary fairy tales. Andersen's work sometimes drew on old folktales, but more often deployed fairytale motifs and plots in new stories; for instance in 'The Little Mermaid', 'The Ugly Duckling' and 'The Emperor's New Clothes.'

Fairy tales are still written in the present day, attesting to their enormous popularity and cultural longevity. Aside from their long and diverse literary history, these stories have also been stunningly illustrated by some of the world's best artists – as the reader will be able to see in the following pages. The Golden Age of Illustration (a period customarily defined as lasting from the latter quarter of the nineteenth century until just after the First World War) produced some of the finest examples of this craft, and the masters of the trade are all collected in this volume, alongside the original, inspiring tales. These images form their own story, evolving in conjunction with the literary development of the tales. Consequently, the illustrations are presented in their own narrative sequence, for the reader to appreciate *in and of themselves*. An introduction to the 'Golden Age' can also be found at the end of this book.

The History of Snow White

The story of *Snow White* is one of the best known and most loved fairy tales. Its history is an intriguing one however, with very little known about its exact origins. The basic narrative involves a young and beautiful woman, who incurs the jealousy of another (whether that be her mother, step-mother, aunt or competing-wife), and as a result is tricked into a state of suspended animation. The young girl is then locked away for her own protection. The story generally ends with the girl rescued and awoken (usually marrying the Prince or the King), and the 'other woman' suffering a less fortunate fate.

This narrative structure first appeared in print (like so many other folkloric tales) in Giambattista Basile's *Pentamerone* (1634-6). Basile was an Italian aristocrat and poet, who had an immense respect for the stories of his homeland. His account of *The Young Slave* demonstrates many of the literary tropes which have since become standard in *Snow White-type* stories. It starts with a beautiful young girl named Lisa, who is cursed by a fairy to die when she is seven years old, due to her mother leaving a comb in her hair. When this happens, her mother places her in seven crystal coffins (the Grimm's later tale has the young woman placed in a glass coffin – with *seven* dwarfs), and locks her in a room. In this narrative, it is the girl's aunt who discovers the room, and jealous of her beauty, pulls her hair, which knocks out the enchanted comb. (Again, this comb motif appears in later tales). The heroine is then mistreated and made to act as a slave, until she is rescued by her uncle, and married to an appropriate suitor. The idea of a child, cursed to sleep in a near-death-like state, and subsequently shut in isolation for their own protection is incredibly old, but 'Snow White' - and of course, 'Sleeping Beauty' are the only tales to utilize this trope directly.

As a testament to this stories popularity and wide geographic reach – the next incarnation of the narrative comes from Indonesia. This time, it is not a prose piece, but a poem believed to have been written around 1750. It is known in the Malay world as *Syair Bidasari* and tells the story of a rich merchant's stunning daughter, who incurred the wrath of the King's wife. Like Basile's *The Young Slave,* Bidasari is ill-treated by the jealous queen, before being placed in a death-like state – this time, by the removal of her enchanted goldfish. The young girl's beauty is unparalleled, described as 'a princess fairer than the day; More like an angel than a mortal maid.' In a fascinating insight into eighteenth century Indonesian concepts of beauty, her cheeks are described as like 'the bill of a flying bird', her nose 'like a jasmine bud', her pretty face like 'the yellow of an egg', and her teeth like 'a bright pomegranate.' This version is also the first tale where the Queen character starts the narrative by asking if there is anyone fairer in the land. The Queen's servants (the dyangs) are reminiscent of the huntsman who takes pity on the young woman, and her isolated palace in the desert is a significant forbear to the house in the woods. Like the poisoned apple being dislodged (or the comb being removed, or the 'stab' being taken out of her finger in the Celtic variant), Bidasari is only awakened when the goldfish is returned.

Despite these two early precedents, it has also been argued that *Snow White* could have been based on a real person. One such possibility is Margarete von Waldeck, who lived in the mid-1500s in a small mining town in north-western Germany. After experiencing troubles with her husband's new wife (so the legend goes), Margarete moved to Brussels, where her beauty attracted the attention of Philip II of Spain. This potential union was deemed unsuitable, and rumour has it that someone poisoned Margarete (her handwriting was shaky enough in her will to suggest tremors due to poison), and she died at the age of twenty-one. There was no happy ending, and no hero-prince for this real life *Snow White.* There is also another historical likelihood – the kind and beautiful 'Maria Sophia Margaretha Catharina von Erthal'. She was born in 1729, so too late for the story of *The Young Slave* and *Bidasari,* but quite possibly an inspiration to the Brothers Grimm (who published *Schneewittchen* in 1812). Historians tell us that Maria's stepmother (Claudia Elizabeth von Erthal) was a domineering woman who clearly favoured her own children, making Maria Sophia's life a misery. Their home, a castle in the heavily forested Lohr region, was also very close to the glass-making industries of the region. Lohr mirrors were famed for their extraordinary quality, with the glass being of such excellence that people said the mirrors 'always spoke the truth.'

Maria's father (Prince Philip), gifted his new-wife one of these looking-glass mirrors, and this very object – quite possibly the inspiration for the Grimms' talking mirror, still survives at the von Erthal castle, which is now a museum. As already noted, the Grimm's *Kinder und Hausmärchen* was first published in 1812, and it was the first tale to incorporate the 'seven dwarfs.' These much loved characters could again have been inspired by the Lohr region, which has seven mountains; most of which were mined. In the mid-eighteenth century, mine tunnels were usually very narrow, so only the smallest of miners (or children) could move around in them. The word the Grimms employ; 'männlein', directly translates as 'little men.' But whilst the 'real life' *Snow Whites* had no fairy-tale ending, *Schneewittchen* is suitably recompensed for her mistreatment. The Grimms' tales often include violent endings (unexpectedly gruesome for many modern readers), and the evil step-mother is forced to wear some red-hot iron shows – in which she must dance until she drops down dead. The Queen also requests to have Schneewittchen's lungs and liver (as proof of her death), which may be a reference to old Slavic mythology, which includes tales of witches eating human hearts.

It was the Grimms' version of the story that 'fixed' the narrative as we know it today, but many other variants existed across Europe. There is the tale of *Myrsina* from Greece, where the sun declares three times that the youngest of three sisters is the most beautiful (inspiring her sibling's jealousy), the story of

Nourie Hadig from Armenia, where the mother asks the Moon, 'Who is the most beautiful in the world', and the Indian epic poem *Padmavati* (1540), where the Queen also asks 'Who is more beautiful, I or Padmavati?' – in this version, she demands the answer from a truth-telling parrot. In the Portuguese narrative (in a similar manner to the German), the Queen requests the young girl's tongue as proof of her death. Analogously to the Huntsman's deception (involving a boar), the servant brings back the tongue of a dog. In a version from Albania, collected by Johann Georg von Hahn (1811 - 1869), the main character lives with forty dragons. Her sleep is caused by a ring, but contains an unusual twist in that a teacher urges the heroine to kill her evil stepmother so that she would take her place.

One particularly intriguing account, is the Celtic story (collected by Joseph Jacobs in 1892) of *Gold Tree and Silver Tree,* where the truth-teller is not a mirror, a parrot, the sun or the moon – but a trout. Unlike all the other narratives, the 'competing wife' in this tale is not jealous of the young girl's beauty (it is her mother, the vain and capricious 'Silver Tree' that plots her downfall) and actually helps 'Gold Tree' escape from her murderous parent. In the Grimm's original version, the step-mother was intended to be the girl's mother, but they pared this aspect down, to make it more suitable for younger readers. In the Celtic variant, the mother manages to strike Gold Tree with a 'poisoned stab', bearing significant resemblance to the thirteenth century *Saga of the Völsungs.* This ancient Icelandic prose narrative tells the story of Brynhild, the beautiful and wise daughter of a famous king, who is punished with eternal slumber after an angered Odin (the ruler of Asgard) struck her with a sleeping thorn. The similarity of these three tales, all from a Northern-European geographic base, is particularly telling in terms of the fairy tale's spread.

As a testament to this story's ability to inspire and entertain generations of readers, *Snow White* continues to influence popular culture internationally, lending plot elements, allusions and tropes to a wide variety of artistic mediums.

The tale has been translated into almost every language across the globe, and very excitingly, is continuing to evolve in the present day. We hope the reader enjoys this collection of some of its best re-tellings.

A certain Queen sat working at a window, the frame of which was made of fine black ebony.
Popular Nursery Stories, 1919.
Illustrated by John Hassall

THE YOUNG SLAVE

(An Italian Tale)

The Young Slave was written by Giambattista Basile (1566 - 1632), a Neapolitan poet and courtier. It was first published in his collection of Neapolitan fairy tales titled *Lo Cunto de li Cunti Overo lo Ttrattenemiento de Peccerille* (translating as 'The Tale of Tales, or Entertainment for Little Ones'), posthumously published in two volumes in 1634 and 1636. Although neglected for some time, the work received a great deal of attention after the Brothers Grimm praised it highly as the first national collection of fairy tales.

Many of the fairy tales that Basile collected are the oldest known variants in existence, including this, the first full-length printed version of a *Snow White–type* narrative. Like later European variants of the story, the 'sleeping beauty' (named Lisa) is placed in seven crystal coffins (akin to the Grimms' glass coffin, and their seven dwarfs), and shut away for her own protection. The story also features a jealous older woman, who discovers the young girl's beauty – and subsequently beats her, treating her as a slave (in a manner akin to the treatment of Bidasari in the Malay epic). Lisa is eventually recognised and rescued however, regaining her health and beauty, and living happily ever after.

>————————>

Jealousy is a fearful malady, and (sooth to say) 'tis a vertigo which turneth the brain, a fever burning in the veins, an accident, a sudden blow which paralyseth the limbs, a dysentery which loos eneth the body, a sickness which robbeth ye of sleep, embittereth all food, cloudeth all peace, shorteneth our days: 'tis a viper which biteth, a moth which gnaweth, gall which embittereth, snow which freezeth, a nail which boreth you, a separator of all love's enjoyments, a divider of matrimony, a dog causing disunion to all love's felicity: 'tis a continual torpedo in the sea of Venus' pleasures, which never doeth a right or good deed: as ye will all confess with your own tongues on hearing the story which follows…

In days of yore, and in times long gone before, there lived a baron of Servascura, and he had a young sister, a damsel of uncommon beauty, who often fared to the gardens in company of other young damsels of her age. One day of the days they went as usual, and beheld a rose-tree which had a beautiful fully-opened rose upon it, and they agreed to wager that whosoever should jump clear above the tree without damaging the rose would win so much. Then the damsels began to jump one after the other, but none could clear the tree; till it coming to Cilia's turn (thus was the baron's sister bight), she took a little longer distance, and ran quickly, and jumped, and cleared the tree without touching the rose, and only a single leaf fell to the ground. She quickly picked it up, and swallowed it before any of the others perceived aught, and thus won the wager.

Three days had hardly passed, when she felt that she was with child, and finding that such was the case she nearly died with grief, well wotting that she had done naught to bring such a catastrophe upon her, and she could not suppose in any way how this had occurred. Therefore she ran to the house of some fairies, her friends, and relating to them her case, they told her that there was no doubt but that she was with child of the leaf she had swallowed. Cilia hearing this hid her state as long as it was possible, but the time came at length for her delivery, and she gave birth secretly to a beauteous woman-child, her face like a moon in her fourteenth night, and she named her Lisa, and sent her to the fairies to be brought up. Now each of the fairies gave to the child a

The Magic Mirror.
My Book of Favourite Fairy Tales, 1921.
Illustrated by Jennie Harbour

The Queen and her Glass.
Grimm's Household Tales, 1912.
Illustrated by R. Anning Bell

charm; but the last of them, wanting to run and see her, in so doing twisted the foot, and for the anguish of pain she felt cursed her, saying that when she should reach her seventh year, her mother in combing her hair would forget the comb sticking in the hair on her head, and this would cause her to die. And years went by till the time came, and the mishap took place, and the wretched mother was in despair at this great misfortune, and after weeping and wailing, ordered seven crystal chests one within the other, and had her child put within them, and then the chest was laid in a distant chamber in the palace; and she kept the key in her pocket. But daily after this her health failed, her cark and care bringing her to the last step of her life; and when she felt her end drawing near, she sent for her brother, and said to him, 'O my brother, I feel death slowly and surely come upon me, therefore I leave to thee all my belongings. Be thou the only lord and master; only must thou take a solemn oath that thou wilt never open the furtherest chamber in this palace, of which I consign to thee the key, which thou wilt keep within thy desk.' Her brother, who loved her dearly, gave her the required promise, and she bade him farewell and died.

After a year had passed the baron took to himself a wife, and being one day invited to a hunt by some of his friends, he gave the palace in charge to his wife, begging her not to open the forbidden chamber, whose key was in his desk. But no sooner had he left the palace than dire suspicion entered in her mind, and turned by jealousy, and fired by curiosity (the first dower of womankind), she took the key, and opened the door, and beheld the seven crystal chests, through which she could perceive a beauteous child, lying as it were in a deep sleep. And she had grown as any other child of her age would, and the chests had lengthened with her. The jealous woman, sighting this charming creature, cried, 'Bravo my priest; key in waistband, and ram within; this is the reason why I was so earnestly begged not to open this door, so that I should not behold Mohammed, whom he worshippeth within these chests.' Thus saying, she pulled her out by the hair of her head; and whilst so doing the comb which her mother had left on her head fell off, and she came again to life, and cried out, 'O mother mine, O mother mine.' Answered the baroness, 'I'll give thee mamma and papa;' and embittered as a slave, and an-angered as a bitch keeping watch on her young, and with poison full as an asp, she at once Cut off the damsel's hair, and gave her a good drubbing, and arrayed her in rags. Every day she beat her on her head, and gave her black eyes, and scratched her face and made her mouth to bleed just as if she had eaten raw pigeons. But when her husband came back and saw this child so badly treated, he asked the reason of such cruelty; and she answered that she was a slave-girl sent her by her aunt, so wicked and perverse that it was necessary to beat her so as to keep her in order.

After a time the baron had occasion to go to a country-fair, and he, being a very noble and kind-hearted lord, asked of all his household people from the highest to the lowest not leaving out even the cats, what thing they would like him to bring for them, and one bade him buy one thing, and another another, till at the last he came to the young slave-girl. But his wife did not act as a Christian should, and said, 'Put this slave in the dozen, and let us do all things within the rule, as we all should like to make water in the same pot; leave her alone and let us not fill her with presumption.' But the lord, being by nature kind, would ask the young slave what she should like him to bring her, and she replied, 'I should like to have a doll, a knife, and some pumice-stone: and if thou shouldst forget it, mayest thou be unable to pass the river which will be in thy way.' And the baron fared forth, and bought all the gifts he had promised to bring, but he forgot that which his niece had bade him bring; and when the lord on his way home came to the river, the river threw up stones, and carried away the trees from the mountain to the shore, and thus cast the basis of fear, and unlifted the wall of wonderment, so that it was impossible for the lord to pass that way; and he at last remembered the curse of the young slave, and turning back, bought her the three things, and then returned home, and gave to each the gifts he had brought. And he gave to Lisa also what pertained to her. As soon as she had her gifts in her possession, she retired in the kitchen,

The Glass answers the Queen a second time.
Grimm's Fairy Tales, 1903.
Illustrated by Helen Stratton

and putting the doll before her, she began to weep, and wail, and lament, telling that inanimate piece of wood the story of her travails, speaking as she would have done to a living being; and perceiving that the doll answered not, she took up the knife and sharpening it on the pumice-stone, said, 'If thou wilt not answer me, I shall kill myself, and thus will end the feast;' and the doll swelled up as a bag-pipe, and at last answered, 'Yes, I did hear thee, I am not deaf.'

Now this went on for several days, till one day the baron, who had one of his portraits hung up near the kitchen, heard all this weeping and talking of the young slave-girl, and wanting to see to whom she spake, he put his eye to the key-hole, and beheld Lisa with the doll before her, to whom she related how her mother had jumped over the rose-tree, how she had swallowed the leaf, how her self had been born, how the fairies had each given her a charm, how the youngest fairy had cursed her, how the comb had been left on her head by her mother, how she had been put within seven crystal chests and shut up in a distant chamber, how her mother had died, and how she had left the key to her brother. Then she spoke of his going a-hunting, and the wife's jealousy, how she disobeyed her husband's behest and entered within the chamber, and how she had cut her hair, and how she treated her like a slave and beat her cruelly, and she wept and lamented saying, 'Answer me, 0 my doll: if not, I shall kill myself with this knife;' and sharpening it on the pumice-stone, she was going to slay herself, when the baron kicked down the door, and snatched the knife out of her hands, and bade her relate to him the story.

When she had ended, he embraced her as his own niece, and led her out of his palace to the house of a relative, where he commanded that she should be well entreated so that she should become cheerful in mind and healthy of body, as owing to the ill-treatment she had endured she had lost all strength and healthful hue. And Lisa, receiving kindly treatment, in a few months became as beautiful as a goddess, and her uncle sent for her to come to his palace, and

Take the child away into the woods and kill her!
Grimm's Fairy Tales, 1898.
Illustrated by E. Stewart Hardy

gave a great banquet in her honour, and presented her to his guests as his niece, and bade Lisa relate to them the story of her past troubles. Hearing the cruelty with which she had been entreated by his wife, all the guests wept. And he bade his wife return to her family, as for her jealousy and unseemly behaviour she was not worthy to be his mate; and after a time gave to his niece a handsome and worthy husband whom she loved.

I will not hurt thee, thou pretty child.
My Book of Favourite Fairy Tales, 1921.
Illustrated by Jennie Harbour

Snow-Drop in the wood.
Popular Nursery Stories, 1919.
Illustrated by John Hassall

BIDASARI

(A Malay Tale)

The following story comes from a romantic Malay poem, believed to have been written around 1750. It gained popularity in the eighteenth and nineteenth centuries, known in the Malay world as *Syair Bidasari,* though it was first mentioned by a Dr. J. Leyden in 1807 as *Hikaiat Bida Sari* (Bidasari Annals). The exact author is unknown, though this particular version was published by Chauncey C. Starkweather (1851 – 1922) in *Malayan Literature; Comprising Romantic Tales, Epic Poetry and Royal Chronicles* (1901). He stated that the exact origin of the tale was again mysterious, though it was likely that it was based 'in the country of Palembang, and its time after the arrival of the Europeans in the Indian archipelago.' (Palembang is the capital city of the South Sumatra province in Indonesia, and Indian trade links with Europe started after the arrival of Vasco da Gama in Calicut, India, on 20th May, 1498.)

The tale of Bidasari bears many striking resemblances to the Grimms' later version of *Snow White,* including the jealous Queen who learns of a young girl fairer than she, her subsequent (failed) attempts to kill Bidasari, and the suspended animation into which Bidasari falls. The Queen's helpers (the dyangs) are also reminiscent of the figure of the huntsman and her isolated palace in the desert is a significant forbear to the house in the woods. Akin to Basile's narrative, where the suspended-animation is caused by an enchanted comb, in this tale, it is an enchanted goldfish. Unlike the Grimms' gruesome ending for the evil step-mother, Lila Sari (the Queen) is not punished, but merely abandoned for her evil actions.

➤

How Neat!
Popular Nursery Stories, 1919.
Illustrated by John Hassall

SONG II

There was once a powerful sultan, who had married the beautiful Lila Sari, making her his Queen. One day, she asked him the following fateful question:

"My noble prince,
   If there were found a woman whose flower face
   Were fairer than all others in the world,
   Say, wouldst thou wed her?" And the King replied:
"My friend, my fairest, who is like to thee?
My soul, my princess, of a noble race,
Thou'rt sweet and wise and good and beautiful.
Thou'rt welded to my heart. No thought of mine
Is separate from thee."

The princess smiled;
Her face was all transfigured with her joy.
But suddenly the thought came to her mind,
"Who knows there is none more fair than I?"
And then she cried: "Now hear me, O my love!
Were there a woman with an angel-face,
Wouldst them make her thy wife? If she appeared
Unto thine eyes more beautiful than I,
Then would thy heart not burn for her?"

The prince
But smiled, and answered not. She also smiled,
But said, "Since thou dost hesitate, I know
That thou wouldst surely wed her." Then the prince
Made answer: "O my heart, gold of my soul,

If she in form and birth were like to thee
I'd join her with thy destiny." Now when
The princess heard these words she paled and shook.

[...]

And swift these thoughts came to her anxious mind:
"I'll seek to-morrow through this kingdom wide,
Lest there should be within the land a maid
More fair than I. To death I shall condemn
Her straight, lest rival she may be to me.
For if my lord should marry her, he'd love
Her more than me. He'd love the younger one,
And constantly my tortured heart would bleed."

On hearing this news, the Queen requests a fan be made of the finest gold and pearls. She orders her servants (the dyangs) to offer it for sale, to all the ladies of the land…

She called the four *dyangs* and said to them:
"A secret mission have I now for ye.
Go up and down among the officers
And show this fan for sale, but never name
The price. Seek ever if there be a face
More beautiful than mine; and should ye find
A face more fair, come tell it straight to me.

After days and days of searching, the servants come to a rich merchant's house. There, they find a beautiful young woman named Bidasari, who wishes to buy the fan…

Towards evening, the Seven Dwarfs came home.
Told Again - Old Tales Told Again, 1927.
Illustrated by A. H. Watson

Now when
The Queen's *dyangs* had looked about them there
They all were dazzled, Bidasari's face
So beautiful appeared. How beat their hearts!
As they upon her lovely features gazed,
Each murmured to herself, "She is more fair
Than our great Queen."

[...]

The four *dyangs* straightway
Departed, hurried to the Queen and said:
"At last we have discovered, O our Queen,
What thou hast sought. 'Tis in a near *campong*
Of merchants very rich and great. Oh, there
We found a princess fairer than the day;
More like an angel than a mortal maid.
No woman in this land compares with her.
Her name is Bidasari. And the King
Would surely marry her if once they met,
For soon she will be ready for a spouse.

[...]

Now when the princess heard them sing her praise
Her soul was wounded as if by a thorn.
Her dark eyes flashed. "Ah, speak no more of her,"
She said, "nor speak abroad what ye have seen.
But bring me Bidasari. I would see
If what ye say be true."

The Seven Dwarfs find Snow-White in their little bed.

Grimm's Fairy Tales, 1917.

Illustrated by Louis Rhead

The Servants eventually manage to persuade Bidasari's parents to let her come to the palace. On seeing the beautiful young girl, the Queen grows angry...

The Queen inclined her head and silence kept,
But wicked thoughts were surging in her brain.
A combat raged within her heart. She feared
The King might see the maiden. "Send away,"
She said, "the nurses and the women all."

Bidasari is locked in a room all alone, and kept there for the night...

[...]

When day appeared,
To the pavilion went the King. The Queen
Threw wide the door of Bidasari's room
And entered all alone.

Then Bidasari
The Queen's hand kissed, and begged that she would let
Her homeward fare. "O gracious Queen," she said,
"Take pity on me; let me go away.
I'll come to thee again."

The wicked Queen
Struck her, and said, "Thou ne'er shalt see again
Thy home." ... The livelong day she was insulted, struck,
And of her food deprived.

The Dwarfs cried out with wonder and astonishment and brought their lamps to look at her and said, "Good heavens! What a lovely child she is."

Grimm's Fairy Tales, 1911.

Illustrated by Charles Folkard

The Seven Dwarfs stood round the sleeper, holding their candles over her to see her better.
Fairy Tales, 1915.
Illustrated by Margaret Tarrant

The Queen's poor treatment of Bidasari continued for many weeks. By this time...

The poor child had lost
Her former color. Black her face had grown
From blows, as if she had been burnt. Her eyes
She could not open. Such her sufferings were
She could not walk. Then unto God she cried:
"O Lord, creator of the land and sea,
I do not know my fault, and yet the Queen
Treats me as guilty of a heinous crime.
I suffer hell on earth. Why must I live?
Oh, let me die now, in the faith, dear Lord.
My soul is troubled and my face is black
With sorrow. Let me die before the dawn.

[...]

All the *dyangs* fair Bidasari's plight
Observed, and kindly pity filled their breasts.
"How cruel is the conduct of the Queen!"
They said. "She made us bring her to her side
But to maltreat the child the livelong day.
It seems as if she wished to slay her quite."
Then secretly they went, with some to watch,
And sprinkled Bidasari's brow. To life
She came, and opened those dear wistful eyes.
"My friends," she said, "I pray ye, let me go
Back home again unto my father's house."

The Queen eventually tries to kill Bidasari, but the young girl instructs her to find a casket where she used to bathe, inside which is a beautiful fish. On sending her servants to fetch the box, the Queen asks...

"Say what signifies
The fish to thee? What shall I do with it?"
Then Bidasari bowed and said: "My soul
Is in that fish. At dawn must thou remove
It from the water, and at night replace.

"Leave it not here and there, but hang it from
Thy neck. If this thou dost, I soon shall die.
My words are true. Neglect no single day
To do as I have said, and in three days
Thou'lt see me dead."

The girl does indeed appear to die - much to the Queens delight. On seeing this, the Queen sends her body back to her parents. The parents react to their daughter's death with an unfathomable grief, as they loved her very much...

The merchant and his wife
Were much disturbed to see at night she came
To life, but when the daylight shone again
They lost her, and her spirit fled away.
This so distressed the merchant's heart, a lone
Retreat he sought to find. The parents cried:
"O dearest child, there's treason in the air.
Hatred and anger the companions are
Of lamentations and of curses dire.
Foul lies for gold are uttered. Men disdain
The promises of God, the faith they owe.

They were very friendly, however, and inquired her name. "Snow-Drop," answered she.
The Fairy Book, 1923.
Illustrated by Warwick Goble

Snow-Drop and the Seven Dwarfs.
A Child's Book of Stories, 1914.
Illustrated by Jessie Willcox Smith

Oh, pardon, God! I ne'er thought the *dyangs*
Would thus conspire. But since they are so bad
And treated Bidasari thus, we'll go
And in the desert find a resting-place.
And may it be a refuge for us all,
Hidden and unapproachable."

Fearful lest the Queen find Bidasari still alive, they take the young maiden to a beautiful palace, hidden away in the remote wilderness, and surrounded by a luscious garden...

SONG III

Hear now a song about the King Djouhan.
The wise and powerful prince e'er followed free
His fancy, and the Princess Lila Sari
Was very happy in her vanity.
Since she had killed (for so she thought) the maid,
Young Bidasari, tainted was her joy.
"The King will never take a second wife,"
She mused, "since Bidasari is now dead."

[...]

Time passed, until one day, the King went on a hunting trip, accompanied by his servants. They happened to stumble upon Bidasari's palace, which the King entered...

Snow-White awoke, and was quite frightened when she saw the seven little men.
Grimm's Fairy Tales, 1936.
Illustrated by Anne Anderson

He saw
Full stretched, upon a bed in dragon's shape,
A human form, in heavy-lidded sleep
That seemed like death, and covered with a cloth
Of blue, whose face betokened deepest grief.
"Is it a child celestial?" thought the King,
"Or doth she feign to sleep? Awake, my sweet,
And let us be good friends and lovers true."
So spake the King, but still no motion saw.
He sat upon the couch, and to himself
He said: "If it a phantom be, why are
The eyes so firmly shut? Perhaps she's dead.
She truly is of origin divine,
Though born a princess." Then he lifted high
The covering delicate that hid the form
Of Bidasari sweet, and stood amazed
At all the magic beauty of her face.
Beside himself, he cried, "Awake, my love."

[...]

When all was dark, sweet Bidasari waked
And saw the King, and tried to flee away.
He seized and kissed her. "Ruby, gold," he said,
"My soul, my life, oh, say, where wouldst thou go?
I've been alone with thee for two whole days,
And all the day thou wrapped in sleep didst lie.
Where wouldst thou go, my dove?" The gentle girl
Was much afraid and trembled.

[...]

Bidasari spoke:

> If thou dost favour me, the Queen will vex
> Her heart. My parents fear her. 'Tis the cause
> Why hither they have brought me. Three long months
> Ago I came, for terror of the Queen."
> She thought on all the horror of those days,
> And choked with sobs, and could no longer talk.

Bidasari, urged on by the King, continued with her story. On finishing her tale...

> A mortal hate
> Then filled the prince's heart against the Queen.
> Touched with deep pity for the maiden young,
> He kissed her once again, and left her there,
> So white and still, as if she lay in death.

[...]

Having rescued Bidasari from her curse of sleep by fetching the beautiful fish (which hung around the Queen's neck), the King builds her a beautiful castle, adorns her with jewels, and the pair marry. One day, Bidasari persuades him to visit his other wife – the old Queen – whom he has now abandoned. Lila Sari reproaches the King for his actions:

> And everywhere thy shame is known, that thou
> Art wedded to a gadabout! Is it
> For princes thus to wed a merchant's child?
> She ought far in the woods to dwell, and know
> Most evil destiny.

Mirror, mirror, hanging there, who in all the land's most fair?

The Red Fairy Book, 1890.

Illustrated by Lancelot Speed

The King but smiled
And said: "If this event is noised abroad,
'Tis thou who wilt receive an evil name.
For who in all the land would dare prevent
The King from marrying? I ought to take
From thee all I have given. But before
The people I've no wish to humble thee.
Is it because I met thy every wish
That thou art grown so bad? Most evil hath
Thy conduct been, and I with thee am wroth,"
And in hot anger rushed the King away,
And straight repaired to Bidasari's side.

In disguise.
Popular Nursery Stories, 1919.
Illustrated by John Hassall

The Dwarfs seeking for gold and silver.
The Big Book of Fairy Tales, 1911.
Illustrated by Charles Robinson

Schneewittchen

(A German Tale)

Schneewittchen ('Little Snow White') is a tale collected by the Brothers Grimm, (or *Die Brüder Grimm*), Jacob (1785–1863) and Wilhelm Grimm (1786–1859). It was first published in *Kinder und Hausmärchen* ('Children's and Household Tales') in 1812. *Kinder und Hausmärchen* was a pioneering collection of German folklore, and the Grimms built their anthology on the conviction that a national identity could be found in popular culture and with the common folk (*Volk*). Their first volumes were highly criticised however, because although they were called 'Children's Tales', they were not regarded as suitable for children, for both their scholarly information and gruesome subject matter.

One such example of this 'unsuitable' subject matter, is the punishment meted out to the evil step-mother. She is forced to put on some red-hot iron shoes, in which she must dance until she dies. The Queen's request to have Snow White's lungs and liver (so that she may eat them), may also be a reference to old Slavic mythology, which includes tales of witches eating human hearts. In the very first edition, the villain was actually Snow White's jealous *mother,* who instead of ordering a servant to take the young girl to the woods, takes her there herself – abandoning her in a manner akin to *Hansel and Gretel.* It is believed that the change to a stepmother in later editions was made in order to tone down the story for children.

It was the middle of winter, and the snow-flakes were falling like feathers from the sky, and a Queen sat at her window working, and her embroidery-frame was of ebony. And as she worked, gazing at times out on the snow, she pricked her finger, and there fell from it three drops of blood on the snow. And when she saw how bright and red it looked, she said to herself, "Oh that I had a child as white as snow, as red as blood, and as black as the wood of the embroidery frame!" Not very long after she had a daughter, with a skin as white as snow, lips as red as blood, and hair as black as ebony, and she was named Snow-white. And when she was born the Queen died.

After a year had gone by the King took another wife, a beautiful woman, but proud and overbearing, and she could not bear to be surpassed in beauty by any one. She had a magic looking-glass, and she used to stand before it, and look in it, and say, "Looking- glass upon the wall, Who is fairest of us all?"

And the looking-glass would answer,

"You are fairest of them all."

And she was contented, for she knew that the looking-glass spoke the truth.

Now, Snow-white was growing prettier and prettier, and when she was seven years old she was as beautiful as day, far more so than the Queen herself. So one day when the Queen went to her mirror and said, "Looking-glass upon the wall, Who is fairest of us all?" it answered,

"Queen, you are full fair, 'tis true, But Snow-white fairer is than you."

This gave the Queen a great shock, and she became yellow and green with envy, and from that hour her heart turned against Snow-white, and she hated her.

Any Laces, my dear? Any necklaces rare?
Alice and Other Fairy Plays for Children, 1880.
Illustrated by Mary Sibree

She showed her pretty stay-laces.
Told Again - Old Tales Told Again, 1927.
Illustrated by A. H. Watson

And envy and pride like ill weeds grew in her heart higher every day, until she had no peace day or night. At last she sent for a huntsman, and said, "Take the child out into the woods, so that I may set eyes on her no more. You must put her to death, and bring me her heart for a token."

The huntsman consented, and led her away; but when he drew his cutlass to pierce Snow-white's innocent heart, she began to weep, and to say, "Oh, dear huntsman, do not take my life; I will go away into the wild wood, and never come home again." And as she was so lovely the huntsman had pity on her, and said, "Away with you then, poor child"; for he thought the wild animals would be sure to devour her, and it was as if a stone had been rolled away from his heart when he did not put her to death. Just at that moment a young wild boar came running by, so he caught and killed it, and taking out its heart, he brought it to the Queen for a token. And it was salted and cooked, and the wicked woman ate it up, thinking that there was an end of Snow-white.

Now, when the poor child found herself quite alone in the wild woods, she felt full of terror, even of the very leaves on the trees, and she did not know what to do for fright. Then she began to run over the sharp stones and through the thorn bushes, and the wild beasts after her, but they did her no harm. She ran as long as her feet would carry her; and when the evening drew near she came to a little house, and she went inside to rest. Everything there was very small, but as pretty and clean as possible. There stood the little table ready laid, and covered with a white cloth, and seven little plates, and seven knives and forks, and drinking cups. By the wall stood seven little beds, side by side, covered with clean white quilts. Snow-white, being very hungry and thirsty, ate from each plate a little porridge and bread, and drank out of each little cup a drop of wine, so as not to finish up one portion alone. After that she felt so tired that she lay down on one of the beds, but it did not seem to suit her; one was too long, another too short, but at last the seventh was quite right; and so she lay down upon it, committed herself to Heaven, and fell asleep.

When it was quite dark, the masters of the house came home. They were seven dwarfs, whose occupation was to dig underground among the mountains.

When they had lighted their seven candles, and it was quite light in the little house, they saw that some one must have been in, as everything was not in the same order in which they left it. The first said, "Who has been sitting in my little chair?" The second said, "Who has been eating from my little plate?" The third said, "Who has been taking my little loaf?" The fourth said, "Who has been tasting my porridge?" The fifth said, "Who has been using my little fork?" The sixth said, "Who has been cutting with my little knife?" The seventh said, "Who has been drinking from my little cup?"

Then the first one, looking round, saw a hollow in his bed, and cried, "Who has been lying on my bed?" And the others came running, and cried, "Some one has been on our beds too!" But when the seventh looked at his bed, he saw little Snow-white lying there asleep. Then he told the others, who came running up, crying out in their astonishment, and holding up their seven little candles to throw a light upon Snow-white.

"O goodness! O gracious!" cried they, "what beautiful child is this?" and were so full of joy to see her that they did not wake her, but let her sleep on. And the seventh dwarf slept with his comrades, an hour at a time with each, until the night had passed. When it was morning, and Snow-white awoke and saw the seven dwarfs, she was very frightened; but they seemed quite friendly, and asked her what her name was, and she told them; and then they asked how she came to be in their house.

And she related to them how her step-mother had wished her to be put to death, and how the huntsman had spared her life, and how she had run the whole day long, until at last she had found their little house

Little Snow-White and the Pedlar-Woman.
Grimm's Fairy Tales, 1898.
Illustrated by Ada Dennis

*The wicked woman laced her so tightly that soon Snowdrop
was unable to breathe and fell down as if dead.*

Fairy Tales, 1915.

Illustrated by Margaret Tarrant

Then the dwarfs said, "If you will keep our house for us, and cook, and wash, and make the beds, and sew and knit, and keep everything tidy and clean, you may stay with us, and you shall lack nothing."

"With all my heart," said Snow-white; and so she stayed, and kept the house in good order. In the morning the dwarfs went to the mountain to dig for gold; in the evening they came home, and their supper had to be ready for them. All the day long the maiden was left alone, and the good little dwarfs warned her, saying, "Beware of your step-mother, she will soon know you are here. Let no one into the house." Now the Queen, having eaten Snow-white's heart, as she supposed, felt quite sure that now she was the first and fairest, and so she came to her mirror, and said,

"Looking-glass upon the wall, Who is fairest of us all?"

And the glass answered,

"Queen, thou art of beauty rare,
But Snow-white living in the glen
With the seven little men
Is a thousand times more fair."

Then she was very angry, for the glass always spoke the truth, and she knew that the huntsman must have deceived her, and that Snow-white must still be living. And she thought and thought how she could manage to make an end of her, for as long as she was not the fairest in the land, envy left her no rest. At last she thought of a plan; she painted her face and dressed herself like an old peddler woman, so that no one would have known her. In this disguise she went across the seven mountains, until she came to the house of the seven little dwarfs, and she knocked at the door and cried, "Fine wares to sell! fine wares to sell!" Snow-white peeped out of the window and cried, "Good-day, good woman, what have you to sell?" "Good wares, fine wares," answered she, "laces of all colors"; and she held up a piece that was woven of variegated silk. "I need not be afraid of letting in this good woman," thought Snow-white, and she unbarred the door and bought the pretty lace. "What a figure you are, child!" said the old woman, "come and let me lace you properly for once." Snow-white, suspecting nothing, stood up before her, and let her lace her with the new lace; but the old woman laced so quickly and tightly that it took Snowwhite's breath away, and she fell down as dead.

"Now you have done with being the fairest," said the old woman as she hastened away.

Not long after that, towards evening, the seven dwarfs came home, and were terrified to see their dear Snow-white lying on the ground, without life or motion; they raised her up, and when they saw how tightly she was laced they cut the lace in two; then she began to draw breath, and little by little she returned to life. When the dwarfs heard what had happened they said, "The old peddler woman was no other than the wicked Queen; you must beware of letting any one in when we are not here!" And when the wicked woman got home she went to her glass and said, "Looking- glass against the wall, Who is fairest of us all?"

And it answered as before,

> "Queen, thou art of beauty rare,
> But Snow-white living in the glen
> With the seven little men
> Is a thousand times more fair."

"There's an end to all thy beauty," said the spiteful Queen, and she went away home.
My Book of Favourite Fairy Tales, 1921.
Illustrated by Jennie Harbour

The poisoned comb.

Popular Nursery Stories, 1919.

Illustrated by John Hassall

When she heard that she was so struck with surprise that all the blood left her heart, for she knew that Snow-white must still be living.

"But now," said she, "I will think of something that will be her ruin." And by witchcraft she made a poisoned comb. Then she dressed herself up to look like another different sort of old woman.

So she went across the seven mountains and came to the house of the seven dwarfs, and knocked at the door and cried, "Good wares to sell! good wares to sell!" Snow-white looked out and said, "Go away, I must not let anybody in." "But you are not forbidden to look," said the old woman, taking out the poisoned comb and holding it up. It pleased the poor child so much that she was tempted to open the door; and when the bargain was made the old woman said, "Now, for once, your hair shall be properly combed."

Poor Snow-white, thinking no harm, let the old woman do as she would, but no sooner was the comb put in her hair than the poison began to work, and the poor girl fell down senseless.

"Now, you paragon of beauty," said the wicked woman, "this is the end of you," and went off. By good luck it was now near evening, and the seven little dwarfs came home. When they saw Snow-white lying on the ground as dead, they thought directly that it was the step-mother's doing, and looked about, found the poisoned comb, and no sooner had they drawn it out of her hair than Snow-white came to herself, and related all that had passed. Then they warned her once more to be on her guard, and never again to let any one in at the door.

They soon found the comb.

European Folk and Fairy Tales, 1913.

Illustrated by John D. Batten

And the Queen went home and stood before the looking-glass and said,

"Looking-glass against the wall, Who is fairest of us all?"

And the looking-glass answered as before,

"Queen, thou art of beauty rare,
But Snow-white living in the glen
With the seven little men
Is a thousand times more fair."

When she heard the looking-glass speak thus she trembled and shook with anger. "Snow-white shall die," cried she, "though it should cost me my own life!" And then she went to a secret lonely chamber, where no one was likely to come, and there she made a poisonous apple. It was beautiful to look upon, being white with red cheeks, so that any one who should see it must long for it, but whoever ate even a little bit of it must die. When the apple was ready she painted her face and clothed herself like a peasant woman, and went across the seven mountains to where the seven dwarfs lived. And when she knocked at the door

Snowwhite put her head out of the window and said, "I dare not let anybody in; the seven dwarfs told me not to." "All right," answered the woman; "I can easily get rid of my apples elsewhere. There, I will give you one." "No," answered Snow-white, "I dare not take anything."

"Are you afraid of poison?" said the woman, "look here, I will cut the apple in two pieces; you shall have the red side, I will have the white one." For the apple was so cunningly made, that all the poison was in the rosy half of it. Snow-white longed for the beautiful apple, and as she saw the peasant woman eating a piece of it she could no longer refrain, but stretched out her hand

and took the poisoned half. But no sooner had she taken a morsel of it into her mouth than she fell to the earth as dead. And the Queen, casting on her a terrible glance, laughed aloud and cried, "As white as snow, as red as blood, as black as ebony! This time the dwarfs will not be able to bring you to life again." And when she went home and asked the looking-glass, "Looking-glass against the wall, Who is fairest of us all?" at last it answered, "You are the fairest now of all." Then her envious heart had peace, as much as an envious heart can have.

The dwarfs, when they came home in the evening, found Snow-white lying on the ground, and there came no breath out of her mouth, and she was dead.

They lifted her up, sought if anything poisonous was to be found, cut her laces, combed her hair, washed her with water and wine, but all was of no avail, the poor child was dead, and remained dead. Then they laid her on a bier, and sat all seven of them round it, and wept and lamented three whole days. And then they would have buried her, but that she looked still as if she were living, with her beautiful blooming cheeks.

So they said, "We cannot hide her away in the black ground." And they had made a coffin of clear glass, so as to be looked into from all sides, and they laid her in it, and wrote in golden letters upon it her name, and that she was a King's daughter. Then they set the coffin out upon the mountain, and one of them always remained by it to watch. And the birds came too, and mourned for Snow-white, first an owl, then a raven, and lastly, a dove.

Now, for a long while Snow-white lay in the coffin and never changed, but looked as if she were asleep, for she was still as white as snow, as red as blood, and her hair was as black as ebony.

Looking-Glass, Looking-Glass on the wall, who is the fairest of women all?
Told Again - Old Tales Told Again, 1927.
Illustrated by A. H. Watson

It happened, however, that one day a King's son rode through the wood and up to the dwarfs' house, which was near it. He saw on the mountain the coffin, and beautiful Snow-white within it, and he read what was written in golden letters upon it. Then he said to the dwarfs, "Let me have the coffin, and I will give you whatever you like to ask for it." But the dwarfs told him that they could not part with it for all the gold in the world. But he said, "I beseech you to give it me, for I cannot live without looking upon Snow-white; if you consent I will bring you to great honor, and care for you as if you were my brethren."

When he so spoke the good little dwarfs had pity upon him and gave him the coffin, and the King's son called his servants and bid them carry it away on their shoulders. Now it happened that as they were going along they stumbled over a bush, and with the shaking the bit of poisoned apple flew out of her throat. It was not long before she opened her eyes, threw up the cover of the coffin, and sat up, alive and well.

"Oh dear! where am I?" cried she. The King's son answered, full of joy, "You are near me," and, relating all that had happened, he said, "I would rather have you than anything in the world; come with me to my father's castle and you shall be my bride." And Snow-white was kind, and went with him, and their wedding was held with pomp and great splendor.

But Snow-white's wicked step-mother was also bidden to the feast, and when she had dressed herself in beautiful clothes she went to her looking-glass and said, "Looking-glass upon the wall, Who is fairest of us all?"

The looking-glass answered,

> "O Queen, although you are of beauty rare,
> The young bride is a thousand times more fair."

Snow-White put her head out of the window.
Grimm's Fairy Tales, 1898.
Illustrated by Ernest Nister

*"Will you not put out," said Silver-Tree,"your little finger through
the keyhole, so that your own mother may give a kiss to it?"*

Celtic Fairy Tales, 1892.

Illustrated by John D. Batten

Then she railed and cursed, and was beside herself with disappointment and anger. First she thought she would not go to the wedding; but then she felt she should have no peace until she went and saw the bride. And when she saw her she knew her for Snow-white, and could not stir from the place for anger and terror. For they had ready red-hot iron shoes, in which she had to dance until she fell down dead.

But scarcely put the piece into her mouth, when she fell down dead.
My Book of Favourite Fairy Tales, 1921.
Illustrated by Jennie Harbour

THE VAIN QUEEN

(A Portuguese Tale)

This story comes from an anthology of *Portuguese Folk Tales*, compiled by Zófimo Consiglieri Pedroso (1851 – 1910), a Portuguese historian, writer, ethnographer and folklorist. He was devoted to the study of ethnography (the systematic study of people and cultures) and introduced anthropology as an academic pursuit to Portugal, studying the country's myths, popular traditions and superstitions. Ironically, for a book dedicated to Portuguese culture and story-telling, the book was actually issued in England (in 1878) *before* its native publication.

In this tale, the vain Queen is actually the beautiful young girl's mother (like the Grimms' proposed first edition). Here, she asks her Chamberlain, instead of a magic mirror, 'is there a face more beautiful than mine?' The attractive daughter in question lives very far away however, and the Queen requests her tongue as proof of her death. Analogously to the Huntsman's deception (involving a boar), the servant in this story brings back the tongue of a dog. There are no dwarfs in Pedroso's account, rather a kindly man who looks after the young woman, providing her with a new life and identity as a peasant girl. It is from his secluded house in the woods, that the Queen has to fetch the young lady (akin to the Dyangs and Bidasari) – unwittingly marrying her to a Prince of the kingdom.

The Dwarfs, when they came in the evening, found Snowdrop lying on the ground.
The Fairy Tales of the Brothers Grimm, 1909.
Illustrated by Arthur Rackham

There was a very vain Queen who, turning towards her maids of honour, asked them, "Is there a face more beautiful than mine?" To which they replied that there was not; and on asking the same question of her servants they made the same answer.

One day she turned towards her chamberlain and asked him, "Is there a more beautiful face than mine?" The chamberlain replied, "Be it known to your august majesty that there is." The queen, on hearing this, desired to know who it could be, and the chamberlain informed her that it was her daughter. The queen then immediately ordered a carriage to be prepared, and placing the princess in it ordered her servants to take her far away into the country and there to cut off her head, and to bring back her tongue.

The servants departed as the Queen had ordered them, but, on arriving at the place agreed upon, they turned towards the princess and said, "Your highness is not aware for what purpose we have brought you here; but we shall do you no harm." They found a small bitch and killed her, and cut her tongue off, telling the princess that they had done this to take it to her majesty, for she had commanded them to behead her, and to take her back the tongue. They then begged of the princess to flee to some distant part and never to return to the city, so as not to betray them.

The maiden departed and went on walking through several lonely wild places until she descried at a distance a small farm-house, and on approaching it she found nothing what ever inside the hut but the trail of some pigs. She walked on, and, on entering the first room she came to, she found a very old chest made of pinewood; in the second room she found a bed with a, very old straw mattress upon it; and in the third room a fire-place and a table. She went to the table, drew open the drawer, and found some food, which she put on the fire to cook. She laid the cloth, and when she was beginning to eat she heard a man coming in.

Her cheeks are still rosy, she looks not like dead.

Alice and Other Fairy Plays for Children, 1880.

Illustrated by Mary Sibree

The maiden, who was very much frightened, hid herself under-the table, but the man, who had seen her hiding away, called her to him. He told her not to be ashamed; and they both afterwards dined at the table, and at night they also supped together. At the end of supper the man asked the princess which she would prefer, to remain as his wife or as his daughter. The princess replied that she should like to remain as his daughter. The man then arranged a separate bed for himself and they each retired to rest. They lived in this way very happily. One day the man told the maiden to go and take a walk to amuse herself. The maiden replied that the dress she wore was too old to go out in, but the man opening a cupboard showed her a complete suit of a country- woman's clothes. The maiden dressed herself in them and went out. When she was out walking she saw a gentleman coming towards her. The maiden immediately turned back very much alarmed, and hid herself at home.

At night when the man returned home he asked her if she had enjoyed her walk, to which she replied that she had, but this she said in a timid tone of voice. The next day the man again sent her out to take a walk. The maiden did so and again saw the same gentleman coming towards her, and as before she fled home in great fright to hide herself. When the man saw her in the evening and asked her whether she had enjoyed her walk the maiden replied that she had not, because she had seen a man approach as though he wished to speak to her, and therefore she did not wish ever to go out again. To this the man made no reply.

The gentleman was a prince, who, on returning twice to the same place, and failing to meet the maiden love-sick. The wisest physicians attended him; and they gave an account of the illness the prince was suffering from. The queen immediately commanded a proclamation to be issued to the effect that the country lass who had seen the prince should at once proceed to the palace, for which she would be recompensed and marry the prince. But as the maiden now never left her home she knew nothing of the proclamation. The queen, seeing that no one presented herself at the palace, sent a guard to search the place. The guard went and knocked at the door, and told the maiden that her majesty sent for her to the palace, and that she would be well rewarded if she came.

The maiden told the guard to return next day for her answer. When she saw the man again in the evening she related to him all that had passed. He told her that when the guard should return for the answer she was to tell him that the queen must come to her as she would not go to the queen. When the guard returned next day for the answer, the girl told him that she did not dare inform him of her decision. The guard told her to say whatever she liked, that he would repeat it to the queen. The girl then told him what the man had advised her to say.

When the guard arrived at the palace he also feared to give the girl's answer; but the queen obliged him to do so. The guard then recounted all that the girl had said. The queen was very angry, but as at that very moment the prince was attacked with a severe fit of convulsions, and the queen feared he might die of it, she resolved to go. She ordered a carriage to be brought and she went to see the maiden; but as she was approaching the house it was transformed into a palace, the man who had sheltered the girl was turned into a powerful emperor, the pigs into dukes, the maiden into a beautiful princess, and all the rest into wealth and riches.

When the queen saw all this she was very much astonished, and made many apologies for having summoned the girl to the palace. She told the maiden that seeing that her son the prince was so greatly in love with her she begged of her, if such was pleasing to her, to consent to marry the prince, as otherwise he would most certainly die. The maiden was willing and acceded to the request of the queen, and the marriage was celebrated with great pomp, and they all lived very happily.

Seven mourners.

Popular Nursery Stories, 1919.

Illustrated by John Hassall

They wrote her name upon it, in golden letters, and that she was a King's.
Hansel and Gretel and Other Stories, 1925.
Illustrated by Kay Nielsen

GOLD TREE AND SILVER TREE

(A Celtic Tale)

Gold Tree and Silver Tree is a story collected by Joseph Jacobs (1854 - 1916) in his *Celtic Fairy Tales* (1892). Jacobs was inspired by the work of the Brothers Grimm and the romantic nationalism common to folklorists of his age; he wished for English children to have access to English fairy tales, whereas they were chiefly reading French and German stories. In his own words, 'What Perrault began, the Grimms completed.'

In this story, the Queen, 'Silver Tree' is jealous of her daughter, 'Gold Tree' (just as *The Vain Queen* was resentful of her beautiful offspring). She is informed of this, not by an enchanted mirror – but by a trout! Akin to other narratives of this type, Silver Tree demands Gold Tree's heart, but is given a fake; that of a goat. On learning that her daughter is still alive, Silver Tree then thrusts a poisoned stab into Gold Tree's finger (like the poisoned apple of the Brothers Grimm). In a similar manner to Basile's early tale of *The Young Slave,* Gold Tree is consequently shut away in her near-death like state, until she is discovered by her husband's new wife, who dislodges the stab and rescues the 'sleeping beauty'. Unlike the jealous wife in the tale of Bidasari though, the other woman actually helps Gold Tree, saving her from her wicked mother – and the three live happily ever after.

One of the Dwarfs sat by it and watched.
Grimm's Fairy Tales, 1903.
Illustrated by Helen Stratton

Once upon a time there was a king who had a wife, whose name was Silver-tree, and a daughter, whose name was Gold-tree. On a certain day of the days, Gold-tree and Silver-tree went to a glen, where there was a well, and in it there was a trout.

Said Silver-tree, "Troutie, bonny little fellow, am not I the most beautiful queen in the world?"

"Oh indeed you are not."

"Who then?"

"Why, Gold-tree, your daughter."

Silver-tree went home, blind with rage. She lay down on the bed, and vowed she would never be well until she could get the heart and the liver of Gold-tree, her daughter, to eat.

At nightfall the king came home, and it was told him that Silver-tree, his wife, was very ill. He went where she was, and asked her what was wrong with her.

"Oh! only a thing which you may heal if you like."

"Oh! indeed there is nothing at all which I could do for you that I would not do."

"If I get the heart and the liver of Gold-tree, my daughter, to eat, I shall be well."

Now it happened about this time that the son of a great king had come from abroad to ask Gold-tree for marrying. The King now agreed to this, and they went abroad.

The king then went and sent his lads to the hunting-hill for a he-goat, and he gave its heart and its liver to his wife to eat; and she rose well and healthy.

A year after this Silver-tree went to the glen, where there was the well in which there was the trout.

"Troutie, bonny little fellow," said she, "am not I the most beautiful queen in the world?"

"Oh! indeed you are not."

"Who then?"

"Why, Gold-tree, your daughter."

"Oh! well, it is long since she was living. It is a year since I ate her heart and liver."

"Oh! indeed she is not dead. She is married to a great prince abroad."

Silver-tree went home, and begged the king to put the long-ship in order, and said, "I am going to see my dear Gold-tree, for it is so long since I saw her." The long-ship was put in order, and they went away.

It was Silver-tree herself that was at the helm, and she steered the ship so well that they were not long at all before they arrived.

Snowdrop lay a long time in the coffin, and she always looked the same, just as if she were asleep.

The Red Fairy Book, 1890.

Illustrated by Lancelot Speed

The Prince saw the glass coffin on the mountain with beautiful Snowdrop lying within.
Fairy Tales, 1915.
Illustrated by Margaret Tarrant

The prince was out hunting on the hills. Gold-tree knew the long-ship of her father coming.

"Oh!" said she to the servants, "my mother is coming, and she will kill me."

"She shall not kill you at all; we will lock you in a room where she cannot get near you."

This is how it was done; and when Silver-tree came ashore, she began to cry out: "Come to meet your own mother, when she comes to see you," Gold-tree said that she could not, that she was locked in the room, and that she could not get out of it.

"Will you not put out," said Silver-tree, "your little finger through the keyhole, so that your own mother may give a kiss to it?"

She put out her little finger, and Silver-tree went and put a poisoned stab in it, and Gold-tree fell dead.

When the prince came home, and found Gold-tree dead, he was in great sorrow, and when he saw how beautiful she was, he did not bury her at all, but he locked her in a room where nobody would get near her.

In the course of time he married again, and the whole house was under the hand of this wife but one room, and he himself always kept the key of that room. On a certain day of the days he forgot to take the key with him, and the second wife got into the room. What did she see there but the most beautiful woman that she ever saw.

She began to turn and try to wake her, and she noticed the poisoned stab in her finger. She took the stab out, and Gold-tree rose alive, as beautiful as she was ever.

At the fall of night the prince came home from the hunting-hill, looking very downcast.

"What gift," said his wife, "would you give me that I could make you laugh?"

"Oh! indeed, nothing could make me laugh, except Gold-tree were to come alive again."

"Well, you'll find her alive down there in the room."

When the prince saw Gold-tree alive he made great rejoicings, and he began to kiss her, and kiss her, and kiss her. Said the second wife, "Since she is the first one you had it is better for you to stick to her, and I will go away."

"Oh! indeed you shall not go away, but I shall have both of you."

At the end of the year, Silver-tree went to the glen, where there was the well, in which there was the trout.

"Troutie, bonny little fellow," said she, "am not I the most beautiful queen in the world?"

"Oh ! indeed you are not."

"Who then?"

"Why, Gold-tree, your daughter."

"Oh! well, she is not alive. It is a year since I put the poisoned stab into her finger."

Where am I?

Grimm's Fairy Tales, 1931.

Illustrated by Ruth Moorwood

"Oh! indeed she is not dead at all, at all."

Silver-tree went home, and begged the king to put the long-ship in order, for that she was going to see her dear Gold-tree, as it was so long since she saw her. The long-ship was put in order, and they went away. It was Silver-tree herself that was at the helm, and she steered the ship so well that they were not long at all before they arrived.

The prince was out hunting on the hills. Gold-tree knew her father's ship coming.

"Oh!" said she, "my mother is coming, and she will kill me."

"Not at all," said the second wife; "we will go down to meet her."

Silver-tree came ashore. "Come down, Gold-tree, love," said she, "for your own mother has come to you with a precious drink."

"It is a custom in this country," said the second wife, "that the person who offers a drink takes a draught out of it first."

Silver-tree put her mouth to it, and the second wife went and struck it so that some of it went down her throat, and she fell dead. They had only to carry her home a dead corpse and bury her.

The prince and his two wives were long alive after this, pleased and peaceful.

I left them there.

Snow White consented, and went home with the Prince.
My Book of Favourite Fairy Tales, 1921.
Illustrated by Jennie Harbour

Pomp and Splendour.
Popular Nursery Stories, 1919.
Illustrated by John Hassall

DEATH OF THE SEVEN DWARFS

(A Swiss Tale)

In this unusual variant of the *Snow White* narrative, we learn of the unfortunate aftermath for the seven dwarfs. The following passage was written down by Ernst Ludwig Rochholz (1809 – 1892) in *Schweizersagen aus dem Aargau,* translating as 'Swiss Legends of Aargau' (published in 1856). Aargau is one of the most northerly cantons of Switzerland, as well as one of the most densely populated regions of the country – perhaps aiding such imaginative story-telling as the one recounted below!

Here, the 'attractive young peasant girl' sleeps with one of the dwarfs in his bed – there being only seven beds, and eight people. (Here, there are similarities with the Celtic account, where the girl is offered a choice of being treated 'as a daughter or wife.' She chooses 'daughter'.) The girl's habitation with the dwarfs causes the outrage of another woman, who thinks that she is 'cohabiting with all seven men.' Consequently, the dwarfs meet their untimely end, and the young girl is never heard of again.

➤——→

On one of the high plains between Brugg and Waldshut, near the Black Forest, seven dwarfs lived together in a small house. Late one evening an attractive young peasant girl, who was lost and hungry, approached them and requested shelter for the night. The dwarfs had only seven beds, and they fell to arguing with one another, for each one wanted to give up his bed for the girl. Finally the oldest one took the girl into his bed.

She was made to get into them and dance till she fell down dead.
The Red Fairy Book, 1890.
Illustrated by Lancelot Speed

Before they could fall asleep a peasant woman appeared before their house, knocked on the door, and asked to be let inside. The girl got up immediately and told the woman that the dwarfs had only seven beds, and that there was no room there for anyone else. With this the woman became very angry and accused the girl of being a slut, thinking that she was cohabiting with all seven men. Threatening to make a quick end to such evil business, she went away in a rage.

That same night she returned with two men, whom she had brought up from the bank of the Rhine. They immediately broke into the house and killed the seven dwarfs. They buried the bodies outside in the garden and burned the house to the ground. No one knows what became of the girl.

THE GOLDEN AGE OF ILLUSTRATION

The 'Golden age of Illustration' refers to a period customarily defined as lasting from the latter quarter of the nineteenth century until just after the First World War. In this period of no more than fifty years the popularity, abundance and most importantly the unprecedented upsurge in quality of illustrated works marked an astounding change in the way that publishers, artists and the general public came to view this hitherto insufficiently esteemed art form.

Until the latter part of the nineteenth century, the work of illustrators was largely proffered anonymously, and in England it was only after Thomas Bewick's pioneering technical advances in wood engraving that it became common to acknowledge the artistic and technical expertise of book and magazine illustrators. Although widely regarded as the patriarch of the *Golden Age*, Walter Crane (1845-1915) started his career as an anonymous illustrator – gradually building his reputation through striking designs, famous for their sharp outlines and flat tints of colour. Like many other great illustrators to follow, Crane operated within many different mediums; a lifelong disciple of William Morris and a member of the Arts and Crafts Movement, he designed all manner of objects including wallpaper, furniture, ceramic ware and even whole interiors. This incredibly important and inclusive phase of British design proved to have a lasting impact on illustration both in the United Kingdom and Europe as well as America.

The artists involved in the Arts and Crafts Movement attempted to counter the ever intruding Industrial Revolution (the first wave of which lasted roughly from 1750-1850) by bringing the values of beautiful and inventive craftsmanship back into the sphere of everyday life. It must be noted that around the turn of the century the boundaries between what would today be termed 'fine art' as opposed to 'crafts' and 'design' were far more fluid and in many cases non-operational, and many illustrators had lucrative painterly careers in addition to their design work. The Romanticism of the *Pre Raphaelite Brotherhood* combined with the intricate curvatures of the *Art Nouveaux* movement provided influential strands running through most illustrators work. The latter especially so for the Scottish illustrator Anne Anderson (1874-1930) as well as the Dutch artist Kay Nielson (1886-1957), who was also inspired by the stunning work of Japanese artists such as Hiroshige.

One of the main accomplishments of nineteenth century illustration lay in its ability to reach far wider numbers than the traditional 'high arts'. In 1892 the American critic William A. Coffin praised the new medium for popularising art; 'more has been done through the medium of illustrated literature... to make the masses of people realise that there is such a thing as art and that it is worth caring about'. Commercially, illustrated publications reached their zenith with the burgeoning 'Gift Book' industry which emerged in the first decade of the twentieth century. The first widely distributed gift book was published in 1905. It comprised of Washington Irving's short story *Rip Van Winkle* with the addition of 51 colour plates by a true master of illustration; Arthur Rackham. Rackham created each plate by first painstakingly drawing his subject in a sinuous pencil line before applying an ink layer – then he used layer upon layer of delicate watercolours to build up the romantic yet calmly ethereal results on which his reputation was constructed. Although Rackham is now one of the most recognisable names in illustration, his delicate palette owed no small debt to Kate Greenaway (1846-1901) – one of the first female illustrators whose pioneering and incredibly subtle use of the watercolour medium resulted in her election to the Royal Institute of Painters in Water Colours in 1889.

The year before Arthur Rackam's illustrations for *Rip Van Winkle* were published, a young and aspiring French artist by the name of Edmund Dulac (1882-1953) came to London and was to create a similarly impressive legacy. His timing could not have been more fortuitous. Several factors converged around the turn of the century which allowed illustrators and publishers alike a far greater freedom of creativity than previously imagined. The origination of the 'colour separation' practice meant that colour images, extremely faithful to the original artwork could be produced on a grand scale. Dulac possessed a rigorously painterly background (more so than his contemporaries) and was hence able to utilise the new technology so as to allow the colour itself to refine and define an object as opposed to the traditional pen and ink line. It has been estimated that in 1876 there was only one 'colour separation' firm in London, but by 1900 this number had rocketed to fifty. This improvement in printing quality also meant a reduction in labour, and coupled with the introduction of new presses and low-cost supplies of paper this meant that publishers could for the first time afford to pay high wages for highly talented artists.

Whilst still in the U.K, no survey of the *Golden Age of Illustration* would be complete without a mention of the Heath-Robinson brothers. Charles Robinson was renowned for his beautifully detached style, whether in pen and ink or sumptuous watercolours. Whilst William (the youngest) was to later garner immense fame for his carefully constructed yet tortuous machines operated by comical, intensely serious attendants. After World War One the Robinson brothers numbered among the few artists of the Golden Age who continued to regularly produce illustrated works. As we move towards the United States, one illustrator - Howard Pyle (1853-1911) stood head and shoulders above his contemporaries as the most distinguished illustrator of the age. From 1880 onwards Pyle illustrated over 100 volumes, yet it was not quantity which ensured his precedence over other American (and European) illustrators, but quality.

Pyle's sumptuous illustrations benefitted from a meticulous composition process livened with rich colour and deep recesses, providing a visual framework in which tales such as *Robin Hood* and *The Four Volumes of the Arthurian Cycle* could come to life. These are publications which remain continuous good sellers up till the present day. His flair and originality combined with a thoroughness of planning and execution were principles which he passed onto his many pupils at the *Drexel Institute of Arts and Sciences*. Two such pupils were Jessie Willcox Smith (1863-1935) who went on to illustrate books such as *The Water Babies* and *At the Back of North Wind* and perhaps most famously Maxfield Parrish (1870-1966) who became famed for luxurious colour (most remarkably demonstrated in his blue paintings) and imaginative designs; practices in no short measure gleaned from his tutor. As an indication of Parrish's popularity, in 1925 it was estimated that one fifth of American households possessed a Parrish reproduction.

As is evident from this brief introduction to the 'Golden Age of Illustration', it was a period of massive technological change and artistic ingenuity. The legacy of this enormously important epoch lives on in the present day – in the continuing popularity and respect afforded to illustrators, graphic and fine artists alike. This *Origins of Fairy Tales from Around the World* series will hopefully provide a fascinating insight into an era of intense historical and creative development, bringing both little known stories, and the art that has accompanied them, back to life.

Other titles in the 'Origins of

Fairy Tales from Around the World' series...

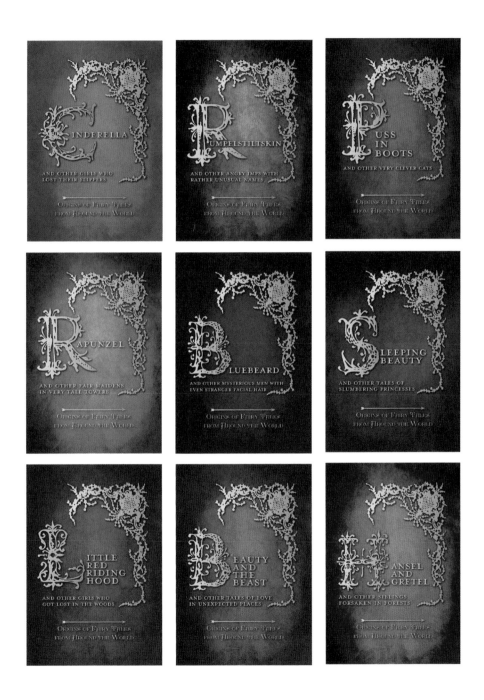

Printed in Great Britain
by Amazon